THOMAS'
Big Book of Beginner Books

THOMAS'
Big Book of
Beginner Books

Based on *The Railway Series* by The Reverend W Awdry

Illustrated by Tommy Stubbs and Owain Bell

RANDOM HOUSE  NEW YORK

Contents

THOMAS'
Big Book of Beginner Books

Stop, Train, Stop!

A Thomas the Tank Engine Story

**Based on *The Railway Series*
by The Reverend W Awdry**

Illustrated by Owain Bell

Every day Thomas the Tank Engine
chugged from the start of his line
to the end of his line
and back again.
"All aboard!"
called the little blue engine's conductor.

Every day Thomas and his coaches
puffed along,
not too fast...
not too slow...
and stopped at every station.

They stopped at Knapford,
where a little boy waved.

KNAPFORD

They stopped at Elsbridge,
where a spotted cow mooed.

15

They stopped at Hackenbeck.
People got on.
People got off.

One morning
the little blue engine said,
"I am tired
of making stops.
I am going to go
from the start of the line
to the end of the line
without stopping."

Clackety-clack!
Clackety-clack!
Away went the train
without looking back.

The little blue engine
whizzed right by Knapford.
The little boy
hardly had time to wave.

In the dining car,
passengers bounced
up and down in their seats.

"Stop, train, stop!
Stop on the spot!
Our hot food's cold
and our cold food's hot!"

But the train didn't stop.
It whizzed right by Elsbridge.
The spotted cow
hardly had time to moo.

In the sleeping car,
passengers bounced
up and down in their beds.

"Stop, train, stop!
Don't go anymore!
Our feet are on the ceiling!
Our heads are on the floor!"

29

But the train didn't stop.
It whizzed right by Hackenbeck.
People could not get on.
People could not get off.

In the baggage car,
trunks and bags and pets
bounced all around.

Splish! A fish splashed
into a cat carrier.

Meow! A cat tumbled
into a bird cage.

Squawk! A bird flew
into a suitcase.
"Stop!" they called.
"Stop, train, stop!"

But the little blue engine
and the long brown coaches
didn't stop until—
SCREECH!—

SCREECH

they reached
the very last station.

The train had gone all the way
from the start of the line
to the end of the line
without stopping once.

The passengers
were not pleased!
Their soup was cold.
Their ice cream was hot.

Dresses were here.
Suits were there.
Fish wagged their tails.
Cats flew everywhere!

And Thomas the Tank Engine
did not feel happy either.
He said, "I miss boys waving.
I miss cows mooing.
I miss people getting on
and people getting off."

So from then on,
every day,
the train
traveled not too fast...
and not too slow...

and stopped at
every station.

"Go, train, go!"

A CRACK IN THE TRACK

Based on *The Railway Series*
by The Reverend W Awdry

Illustrated by Tommy Stubbs

Thomas was a little blue steam engine.
He lived on the Island of Sodor
with many other engines.

Sometimes Thomas pulled his coaches,
Annie and Clarabel.

"Hurry, hurry!" said the coaches.

Sometimes Thomas pulled freight cars.

"Faster, faster!" said the foolish freight cars.

They would try to push Thomas down the hill.

And sometimes Thomas traveled
all by himself across the island.

He chugged in the rain.

He huffed in the sun.

And he puffed in the snow.

"There is nothing a train cannot do!"
Thomas said proudly.

One morning, Henry the Green Engine
would not come out of his shed.
He had boiler ache.

So Sir Topham Hatt asked Thomas to help.

"Peep, peep," Thomas said to the people.

"I can take you where you want to go!"

Soon clouds gathered.

The sky grew dark.

Thunder rumbled.

Plip. Plop. CLUNK.

Hail began to fall!

It fell on Thomas.

It fell on the tracks.

Suddenly, Thomas' driver
saw trouble ahead.
"Slow down!" said the driver.

The hail had made a crack
right there in the track!
Thomas came to a stop.
His driver called out,
"We cannot go forward,
and we must not go back."

"Everyone off!" the conductor said.

"Now what shall we do?"
said the people.

They climbed down from the coaches
and climbed up to the road.
Bertie the Bus was just passing by.

Bertie beeped his horn merrily.

"A bus is as good as a train!" he said.

"I can take you where you want to go!"

All the people climbed on board Bertie.

Bertie scooted down the road.

"A bus *is* as good as a train,"

the people said.

Suddenly, Bertie's driver
saw trouble ahead.
"Slow down!" the driver said.

There in the road
was a bright green toad.
Bertie came to a stop.
His driver called out,
"There's a toad in the road!
We will have to unload."

"Everyone off!" said Bertie's driver.
(That toad in the road
caused a fuss on the bus.)

"What will happen to us?"
the people said.

Then they walked down the road
to another train station.

But the trains were not running.

"Why not?" asked the people.

They soon found out.

Thomas was still stuck
at the crack in the track.
Percy was stuck there at Thomas' back.

Gordon was stuck
behind Thomas and Percy.

James, with two freight cars,
was in quite a hurry.

The freight cars were needed in the yard.
But James could not get past
Gordon and Percy and Thomas.

And the foolish freight cars refused
to back up.
"No, no, no!" they said.
"We will not go!" they said.

So no trains could move up.

And no trains could move back.

They were stuck where they were
at that crack in the track!

"I guess there are some things
that a train cannot do," said Thomas' driver.
"We need help," said Thomas.
"And I know just who to call."

Thomas' driver called Sir Topham Hatt
and told him Thomas' plan.
"An excellent plan!" Sir Topham said.
"Please thank Thomas," he added.

In no time at all,
Harold the Helicopter
zoomed across the sky.

He landed near the people.

They all climbed aboard.

"A helicopter is

as good as a train!" said Harold.

"I can take you

where you want to go!"

The breakdown crew came
to replace the broken track.
By the time they arrived,
rain was falling hard.

The crew came with cranes.

They sang while they worked.

"A crane is as good

as a bus or a train.

We'll fix up your track,

and we don't mind the rain."

Finally, Thomas could move.
So could Percy and Gordon.
James, with his freight cars,
was close behind.

They turned on the turntable
and went back to work.

The people saw Thomas
waiting to take them home.
"Are you *sure* you can take us
where we want to go?" they asked.

"I thought there was nothing
a train could not do," said Thomas.
"But now I know that just isn't true.
I learned a big lesson from one little crack.
A train is only as good as its track."

Go, Train, Go!

A Thomas the Tank Engine Story

Based on *The Railway Series*
by The Reverend W Awdry

Illustrated by Tommy Stubbs

Here comes the judge
in her big red hat.
She has come to see the train show.
Who will take the judge to the train show?

Thomas will!

Thomas will go.

Thomas will take the judge to the show.

"Hurry, Thomas! Take me to the show.
Take me there fast. Go, train, go!"
Clickety-clack, clickety-clack,
up, up the hill,
Thomas the Tank Engine
goes faster than fast.

Screech! go the brakes.

Thomas goes so slow.

Slow,

slow,

slower

than slow he goes.

"Hurry, Thomas! Why do you go so slow?

Take me to the train show. Go, train, go!"

But Thomas cannot go.

Thomas sees a goat.

The goat is on the track.

Peep! Peep! goes Thomas.

Baaaa! The goat jumps back.

Clickety-clack, clickety-clack,
down, down the hill,
Thomas the Tank Engine
goes faster than fast.

Screech! go the brakes.

Thomas goes so slow.

Slow,

slow,

slower

than slow he goes.

"Hurry, Thomas! Why do you go so slow?
Take me to the train show. Go, train, go!"

The tunnel is so dark.
Slow, slow, slow
he goes
into the dark,
      dark,
           dark
               tunnel . . .

. . . and out the other side!

Clickety-clack, clickety-clack,
over a bridge.
He was going so fast.

He was going so fast,
the judge lost her hat!

Screech! go the brakes.

Thomas goes slow.

Slow,

slow,

slow

he goes.

"Hurry, Thomas!
We're running late, you know.
Take me to the train show.
Go, train, go!"

But Thomas must go slow.

There is a cow on the track.

Moo! Moo! goes the cow.

Peep! Peep! goes Thomas.

The cow moves back.
Clickety-clack, clickety-clack,
Thomas the Tank Engine
moves faster than fast!

Screech! go the brakes.

Thomas goes slow.

Slow,

slow,

slow

he goes.

"Don't stop, Thomas. Go, train, go!

Don't stop now. I'm late for the show!"

But Thomas must go slow.

There are logs on the track.

The crane engine clears the logs.
Clickety-clack, clickety-clack,
around the logs goes Thomas,
faster than fast.

There is mud up ahead!

The judge wants to go slow.

"Slow, little engine.

Slow, slow, slow.

Watch out for the mud!

Whoa, train, whoa!"

But Thomas cannot go slow.

Thomas goes faster than fast.

Into the mud . . .

Splish! Splash!

Thomas goes fast.

Past a town,

fast, fast.

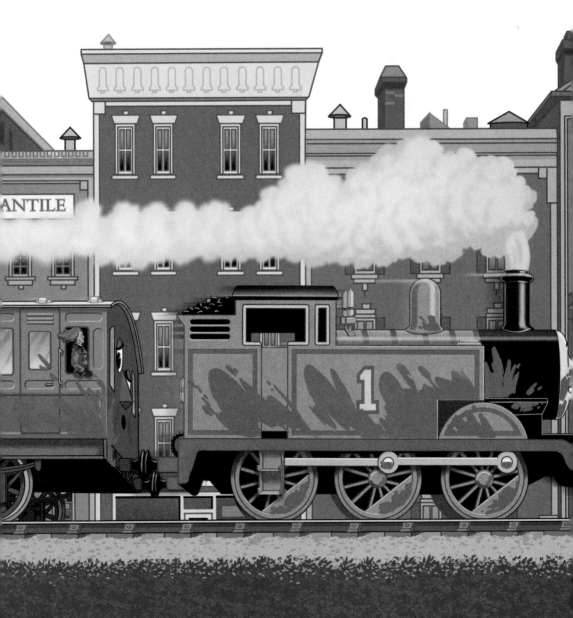

Past a dog,
faster still.
Fast at last!

Nothing can stop him,
nothing at all.
No goat.
No dark.

No cow.

No log.

No crane.

No mud.

No town.

No dog.

This is the fastest

that Thomas can go!

Screech! go the brakes.

"Good job, Thomas!
We made it here at last!
You are a little engine,
but you go so fast!"

Here comes the judge!

The train show begins.

There are red trains and blue trains
and old trains and new trains.
And a little blue engine covered in mud.
What will the judge say?

"I like all the trains. You all are such fun.
But the muddy little blue train
is my favorite one."

Blue Train, Green Train

Based on *The Railway Series*
by The Reverend W Awdry

Illustrated by Tommy Stubbs

Up comes the yellow sun!
Blue train Thomas starts his run.

Green train Percy sees the sun.
Now his busy run is done.

Well done, green train!
Have fun, blue train!

"Peep! Peep!" Clickety-clack!
Blue train Thomas on the track.

Load up the brown cows,

white eggs, green plows.

Load up the blue bikes,
red wagons, orange trikes!

Load up the new toys,

gifts for little girls and boys!

The sun is yellow.
The sun is round.
The sun makes shadows
on the ground.

Here comes a gray cloud!
Blue train Thomas peeps so loud.

Down, down on the train,
gray clouds start to rain.
"Peep! Peep! Oh, no!"
Where can wet train Thomas go?

"Peep, peep!" The sun is back.
Blue train slows down on the track.
Unload the brown cows,
white eggs, green plows.

Unload the blue bikes,
red wagons, orange trikes!
Unload the new toys
for happy little girls and boys!

Down goes the yellow sun.
Blue train Thomas' day is done.
Home now to the Shed.
"Peep, peep!"
The Shed is where
Thomas can sleep.

Up peeps the white moon.
Green train starts soon.
"Peep! Peep!" Clickety-clack!
Green train Percy on the
track.

Load up all the mail
and unload along the rail.

Boxes of all shapes and sizes.
Blue presents, red prizes.

Cards and letters by the sack.
Lots of brown crates in a stack.

Green train Percy slows down.
He picks some up
and puts some down.
Boxes of all shapes and sizes.
Blue presents, red prizes.
Cards and letters by the sack.
Lots of brown crates in a stack.

The moon is round.
The moon is white.
The moon makes shadows
in the night.

The night is cool.
The fog is thick.
A yellow light
will do the trick.

Up peeps the yellow sun!
Green train Percy now is done.
Home now to the Shed.
"Peep, peep!"
The Shed is where
Percy can sleep.

Blue train sees the sun.
Time again to start his run!

Well done, green train.

Have fun, blue train.

Trains, Cranes & Troublesome Trucks

A Thomas & Friends Story

Based on *The Railway Series*
by The Reverend W Awdry

Illustrated by Tommy Stubbs

The sun comes up on trains and cranes
of many different sizes.

The Troublesome Trucks are also up . . .
up to no-good surprises.

Thomas, James, and Gordon
each must make a harbor run.
Small, medium, and big loads,
a job for everyone.
But the Troublesome Trucks
just want to have fun, fun, fun!

Today small Thomas has a goal.

Today he pulls dusty coal.

Thomas must go slow, slow, slow.

The Troublesome Trucks want to go, go, go!

Thomas peeps, "No, no, no!"

The Trucks push Thomas faster, faster.

The curve ahead could mean disaster.

Go, go, go, down the hill.

CRASH!

Oh, what a great big spill!

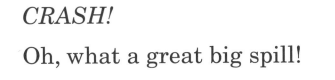

Thomas is off the track.
Harvey comes to lift him back.
Small engine, big trouble.
Small crane helps on the double.
Thomas can only grin and sigh
as James comes rushing by.

Medium-sized James pulls milk today.

He has no time to talk or play.

James must go slow, slow, slow.

The Troublesome Trucks want to go, go, go!

James toots, "No, no, no!"

The Trucks brake hard and then let go.

A jerky, jumpy ride. Oh, no!

They rock and roll, and with a . . .

SPLASH!

James has a great big crash!

Poor James is off the track.

Rocky comes to lift him back.

Medium engine, big trouble.

Medium crane helps on the double.

James can only grin and sigh

as Gordon comes rushing by.

Gordon is big. He pulls heavy freight.

He must be careful and not be late.

Gordon must go slow, slow, slow.

The Troublesome Trucks want to go, go, go!

Gordon chuffs, "No, no, no!"

Down to the Docks, they rush without care.
Before they know it, they are there.
At the end of the line, Gordon cannot stop.

BANG!

Into the bumper, the Trucks flip-flop.

Poor Gordon is off the track.

Cranky is there to lift him back.

Big engine, BIG trouble.

Big crane helps on the double.

Gordon can only sigh and grin

as James and Thomas both pull in.

Thomas, James, and Gordon
go back to the Yard.
Three dirty engines
have all worked hard.

They grumble, grumble, grumble
about those Troublesome Trucks.

Splish, splosh, splash.

Workers wash each one.

Small, medium, big—

the washing-up is fun.

Rub them down and make them shine . . .

then back to the Shed, looking fine.

The sun goes down on Thomas and friends.

A lesson was learned in the end.

When Trucks cause trouble,

just call on the cranes—

they are there on the double

to help all sizes of trains.

Fast Train, Slow Train

Based on *The Railway Series*
by The Reverend W Awdry

Illustrated by Tommy Stubbs

James is off to Ballahoo.
Edward has to go there, too.

James thinks that he's so fine—
the fastest racer on the line.
James says he wants to race.
Edward makes a funny face.

James sets off.
Go, go, go!

Edward follows—
so, so slow.

James races. Clickety-clack.
Edward chugs on down the track.

Look! A cow! James races past.
He's a racer, racing fast.

Edward slows down for the cow.
Does she need his help somehow?

Look! A calf is on the track.
Edward stops to get it back.

James races. Clickety-clack.
Edward chugs on down the track.

Look! It's Percy!
Stuck on the track.

James races on.
Edward holds back!

Edward helps a friend in need.

Racing James keeps the lead.

Bertie is stuck.
He is out of gas.
He needs help.
James races past.

Edward slows and
then he stops.

He takes some shoppers
to the shops.

James thinks he is the best.
He's way ahead. He can rest.
He sees that he is bright and clean
in his reflection in the stream.

James thinks he is the better train.
Isn't he a little vain?

James does not see
Edward chug past.

But now it is James
who is the last.

Edward gets to Ballahoo.
He is slow and Really Useful, too.

James the racer lost the race.
Vanity won him second place.

About the Author

Thomas the Tank Engine first appeared in the early 1940s, when the Reverend W Awdry lovingly crafted a small blue train engine made of wood for his son Christopher. The stories that he made up to accompany the wonderful toy were first published in 1945. In the years since, generations of children and their families have come to know and love Thomas and his many friends on the imaginary Island of Sodor through the many books written about them.

During his own childhood in England, the Reverend Awdry would lie in bed at night listening to the trains of the Great Western Railway that ran along tracks close to his home. He would imagine all the engines talking with one another and invented characters for them. It was these engines and their imagined characters that inspired the Reverend to write the original books in the Railway Series. Today, children the world over can embark on adventures with Thomas & Friends through timeless stories that gently emphasize the importance of friendship, kindness, cooperation, and the wonders of discovery.